BEATRIX POTTER AND PETER RABBIT

BEATRIX POTTER AND PETER RABBIT

Text by Nicole Savy
and Diana Syrat

FREDERICK WARNE

This book was first published for the exhibition *Pierre Lapin au Musée d'Orsay*, held at the Musée d'Orsay, Paris, from September 1992 to January 1993.

FREDERICK WARNE

Published by the Penguin Group
Penguin Books Ltd, 27 Wrights Lane, London W8 5TZ, England
Penguin Books USA Inc., 375 Hudson Street, New York, N.Y. 10014, USA
Penguin Books Australia Ltd, Ringwood, Victoria, Australia
Penguin Books Canada Ltd, 10 Alcorn Avenue, Toronto, Ontario, Canada M4V 3B2
Penguin Books (N.Z.) Ltd, 182-190 Wairau Road, Auckland 10, New Zealand

Penguin Books Ltd, Registered Offices: Harmondsworth, Middlesex, England

First published in French by Editions Gallimard and Réunion des Musées Nationaux 1992
This edition first published 1993 by Frederick Warne
3 5 7 9 10 8 6 4 2

This edition with new reproductions of Beatrix Potter's book illustrations first published 1993

ISBN 0 7232 4215 1

Printed and bound in Great Britain by
William Clowes Limited, Beccles and London

*Beatrix
aged nine*

Beatrix Potter was born in London in 1866.
She lived in a large house in an elegant
square called Bolton Gardens. Her father
was a lawyer with plenty of money and

servants to run the home. Like many children at that time, Beatrix saw very little of her parents and was looked after instead by a nanny. She had a brother, Bertram, who was born when she was six. Although he was so much younger than her they were very good friends.

Bolton Gardens in November, painted by Beatrix

Beatrix did not go to school but was taught at home by a governess. She and Bertram spent most of their time in the schoolroom at the top of the house, and Beatrix rarely saw any other children. However, she was not unhappy. Her parents, though strict about many things, didn't mind her keeping all kinds of pet animals in the schoolroom. At different times she and Bertram had rabbits, mice, lizards, a snake, a bat, a frog

A portrait of a rabbit, drawn when Beatrix was thirteen

Beatrix's lizard, Judy

and a tortoise. And they sometimes did exciting experiments, such as skinning and boiling a dead rabbit to study its skeleton.

*One of
Beatrix's
first
sketchbooks*

Beatrix also loved painting. Her parents arranged for a drawing teacher to come to the house to give her lessons.

*A page of
caterpillars*

When she was older her father took her to visit art galleries and she met some of his artist friends, including the painter John Millais.

John Millais in his studio

But Beatrix taught herself a lot about painting by watching her pets carefully and drawing them as realistically as she could.

The view from Camfield Place

Mr and Mrs Potter enjoyed going on holiday to the country and this was another great pleasure for Beatrix. One of her favourite places was her grandmother's house, Camfield Place in Hertfordshire, where they often stayed. Beatrix loved the

large grounds full of old trees, and the fresh
farm milk and eggs her grandmother had
for tea.

*Beatrix's
bedroom at
her grand-
mother's
house*

During the summer the Potters sometimes spent as long as three months in the country. Mr Potter liked fishing and used to rent a large house by a river in Scotland. The whole family plus all the servants and animals made the journey north by train. Even Beatrix's smaller creatures, such as rabbits and lizards, travelled in boxes.

Beatrix with her dog Spot in Scotland

*A
wood-
mouse*

The wild, mountainous scenery of Scotland
was as different as possible from the busy,
noisy streets Beatrix was used to. She and
Bertram were able to spend hours
exploring the countryside.

*A baby
hedgehog*

The Potter family at Wray Castle

When Beatrix was sixteen, Mr Potter chose
a new place for their summer holiday, the
English Lake District. He leased Wray
Castle, a very grand building by a lake.
Beatrix thought the Lake District was the
most beautiful place she had ever seen and
she longed to live there.

In London, although Beatrix was often alone, she was never bored. She wrote a diary in a secret code in which she described all the things that happened to her and how she hoped that she would be a real artist one day.

Beatrix's diary in code

However, there was no question of a young girl, in the days of Queen Victoria, taking a job. Even when she was grown up, she was expected to stay quietly at home with her parents. To occupy herself she worked very hard at her painting and studied plants and insects. She became especially interested in

A study of mushrooms

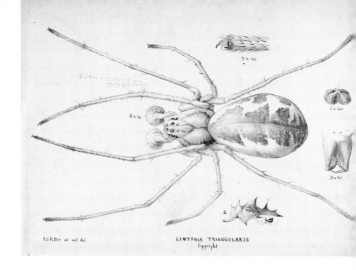

spider, enlarged under a microscope

...ushrooms and discovered new facts about
...ow they grow. She began to think she would
...ke to be a scientist, but the experts of the
...me did not want to take seriously the work of
...young woman.

One of Beatrix's Christmas cards

Disappointed, Beatrix consoled herself by painting pictures for fun showing her pet animals dressed as people. She had a lively rabbit called Benjamin, who would rush up when the bell

A happy New Year to you.

Studies of Benjamin's head

24

An illustration for Cinderella

rang for tea and eat buttered toast, and he
was her favourite model. Her paintings
were admired because the animals were so
lifelike. She spent hours doing little
sketches of Benjamin's head or his feet until
they were just right. She also drew her own
illustrations for fairy stories and rhymes.
She was able to sell some of her pictures to
make greetings cards and this success gave
her new hope.

Beatrix also loved telling stories. In September 1893, when she was on holiday in Scotland, she sent a letter to a young friend, a boy called Noel. He was ill and to cheer him up she wrote him a story

Beatrix aged twenty-five, with Benjamin on a lead

The Peter Rabbit picture letter

with little pictures all about the adventures of another of her pet rabbits, Peter.

The real Peter Rabbit

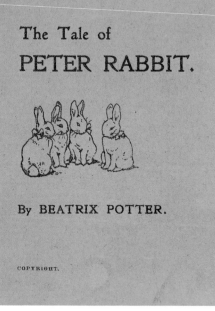

The
*privately-
printed
edition*

Noel liked the story so much that Beatrix decided to make it into a book. She drew black and white pictures for every page and paid to have it printed herself. Then, in 1902, a company in London, Frederick Warne, offered to publish it for her if she would do all the drawings in colour. This new version of *The Tale of Peter Rabbit* immediately sold thousands of copies and became one of the bestselling children's stories ever written.

The first edition published by Warne

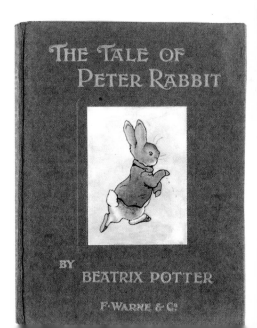

Beatrix wrote more books. She was now earning her own money as an author and didn't have to depend on her parents for everything. She decided to buy a little farm called Hill Top in a village in the Lake

Beatrix's village in winter

A Lake District farm in The Tale of Pigling Bland

District, which had always remained her favourite place. She spent as much time there as she could when she wasn't needed by her parents, and she often drew Hill Top as the background for her tales.

Beatrix and William on their wedding day

She grew very interested in farming and soon bought a second farm nearby. She had a friend, William Heelis, who helped her with the business of buying land. He and Beatrix became very fond of each other and he asked her to marry him. So at last, at the age of 47, she left London for good and settled in the Lake District with her new husband.

Beatrix at a show with her sheep

With William's help she became a real sheep-farmer. She kept large flocks of the best Lake District breed, and frequently won prizes for her sheep at the country shows.

Jemima Puddle-duck in a Lake District landscape

*Beatrix aged
seventy-seven*

Beatrix continued to buy land, and she was
determined to preserve the beauty and peace
of the lovely countryside. She worked with
the organization called the National Trust
which saves attractive places from being
destroyed or built on. By the time she died
in 1943, aged 77, she had bought over 4,000

34

acres of land in the Lake District, and in her will she left it all to the National Trust so that it should remain undeveloped and unspoilt for ever.

Benjamin Bunny's father

It was thanks to the popularity of her little books that Beatrix had money to spend on saving the countryside. There were eventually twenty-three titles in the Peter Rabbit series, all inspired by real animals and country places Beatrix loved. Benjamin Bunny and the Flopsy Bunnies are based on Beatrix's pets. Mr. Jeremy Fisher, the frog, lives by a lake with waterlilies, just like the lake near Hill Top.

Mr. Jeremy Fisher

Beatrix's painting of waterlilies

Mrs. Tiggy-winkle was Beatrix's own hedgehog who was used to lying still while Beatrix drew her. (Although, when she was bored she would begin to yawn, and if Beatrix went on drawing she would bite!)

An unfinished sketch of Mrs. Tiggy-winkle

Mrs. Tabitha Twitchit looking for her son Tom on the stairs at Hill Top

The Tale of Tom Kitten and *Samuel Whiskers* are set at Hill Top and show pictures of the house and farm looking exactly as they do today.

The first French edition

The stories of Peter Rabbit and his friends quickly became popular all over the world.

A music book

Mrs. Rabbit giving Peter camomile tea – a special greetings card design

They were translated into many languages, from French to Japanese and even Latin! Beatrix also produced painting and music books and a Peter Rabbit board game. She agreed that his picture could be used on all kinds of articles, from handkerchiefs to wallpaper. Today you can drink out of a Peter Rabbit cup or sleep in Peter Rabbit pyjamas.

*The amiable
guinea-pig*

By the end of her life Beatrix Potter was
rich and famous. But she hated publicity
and always lived quietly among her farm
animals, enjoying the scenery and creatures
who had inspired her books and her
paintings. Her hope was that her stories
would help other people to appreciate the
beauty of the natural world which had given
so much pleasure to her.

*Old Mr.
Pricklepin*

Three little mice

ACKNOWLEDGEMENTS

Illustrations and photographs in this
book are reproduced by courtesy
of the following:

*National Art Library, Victoria and
Albert Museum*, pages 10, 11, 12, 13,
14, 15, 16, 17, 18, 19 (below), 20, 21,
22, 23, 24, 25, 27 (below), 30, 31,
37 (below), 38, 39, 42, 43

*Trustees of the Linder Collection,
Book Trust*, page 19 (above)

Frederick Warne Archive, pages 26,
27 (above), 28, 29, 33, 34, 40, 41

Private collection, page 32